About the Author

Brian Bird has spent most of his working life as an electrical test engineer, before deciding to become an author. He came up with the story of Haley-Ann the Alien whilst up a ladder and started to type the book on his mobile phone.

He is married with two children and for many years has written funny rhymes for his own children's entertainment, before deciding to write stories for others to enjoy.

Dedication

I would like to dedicate this book firstly to my wife, two sons and one angel in heaven. You bring so much joy into my life every day and inspire me in my writing. I thank you for all your patience, love and support.

Also to the rest of my family and friends I would like to thank you for all your support and advice. You've all been 'out of this world!'

Brian Bird

HALEY-ANN THE ALIEN

AUSTIN MACAULEY
PUBLISHERS LTD.

A CIP catalogue record for this title is available from the British Library.

ISBN 9781786291837 (Paperback)

ISBN 9781786291844 (Hardback)

ISBN 9781786291851 (E-Book)

www.austinmacauley.com

First Published (2017)

Austin Macauley Publishers Ltd.

25 Canada Square

Canary Wharf

London

E14 5LQ

Acknowledgments

I would like to thank my publisher Austin Macauley for giving me this opportunity to share my story with children everywhere.

To everyone who has purchased this book: I thank you 'to the moon and stars and back again'.

From far beyond, in deepest space,
There lived a creature,
from another place.

It wasn't a girl and it wasn't a man,
But it had a name, which was
Haley-Ann.

Now to say
what she looks like is not easy to do,
As her body was red and her head was
blue!

She had ten toes,
nothing strange you may think,
Until I tell you,
these were used to eat food and to drink!

Her nose was long just like an elephant's trunk, She had a black and white tail that resembled a skunk!

Standing at three metres high and weighing more than a ton, When she backfired it sounded a lot like a gun!

Now the planet she lived on was a lonely old place.

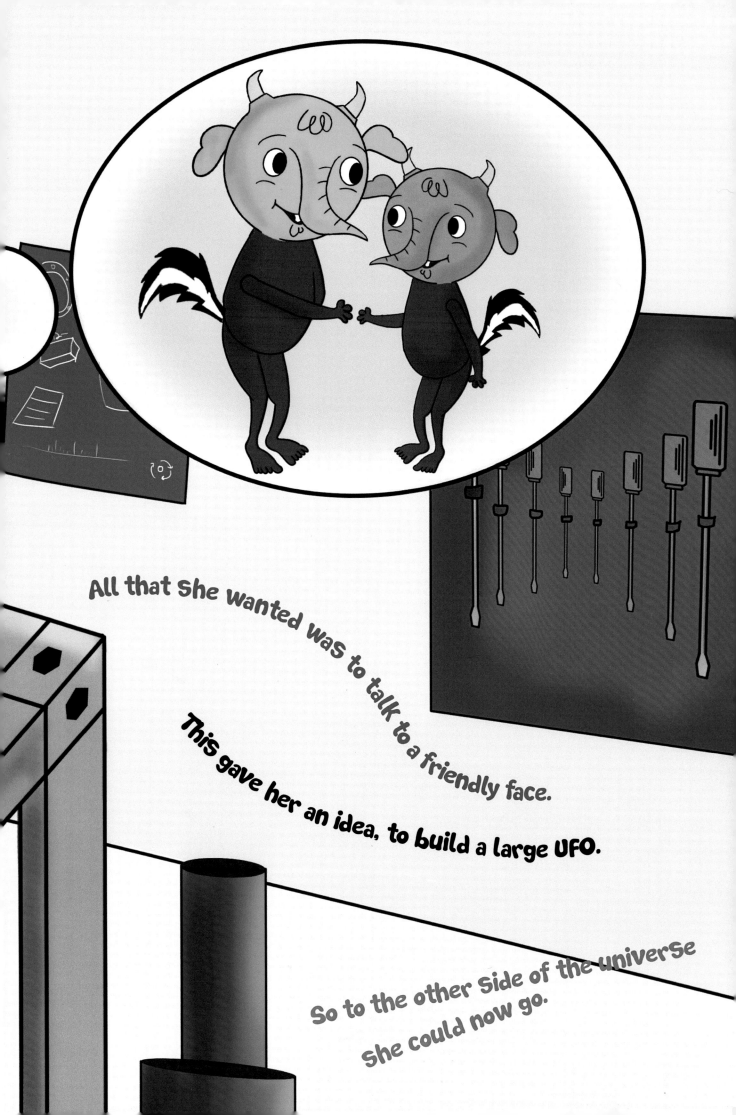

All that she wanted was to talk to a friendly face.

This gave her an idea, to build a large UFO.

So to the other side of the universe she could now go.

After
more than a year,
the **Spaceship** was ready to fly.
She bid farewell to her planet
and waved it
goodbye.

WORK SHOP

OIL

012

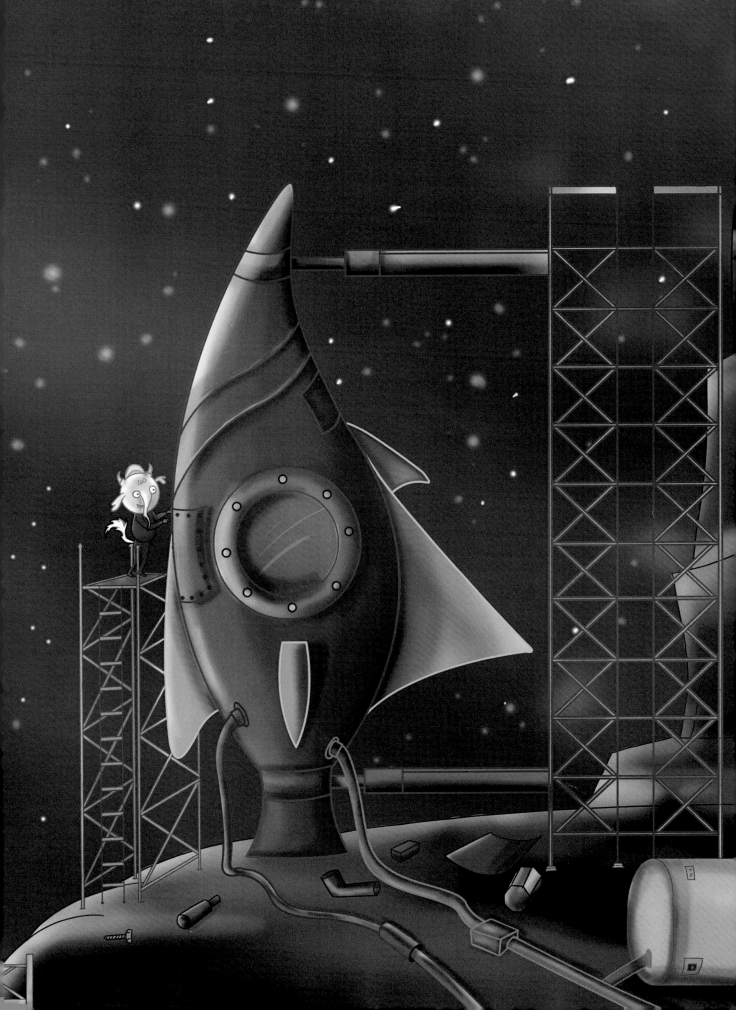

With a roar from the engines,
she was then gone!

Travelling faster
than the speed of light,
The galaxy's colours were a
breathtaking Sight!

The computer **BEEPED** and the craft braked to a halt. Haley-Ann looked **PUZZLED,** "Why, there must be a fault!"

She stared out the window,
for what good it was worth
and glared at a blue and green ball
called 'planet Earth'.

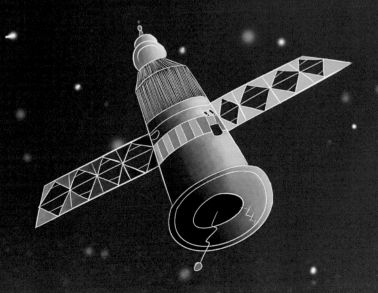

After reprogramming the **UFO**
to find a good place to land
It finally blasted down on some hot,
dry desert sand.

Haley-Ann opened the door and
glanced all around.
There was nobody here on this planet
she'd found.

Just then came over an odd looking, two **humped mammal**, who introduced himself as

HUMPHREY the camel.

"Hello," he muttered,
"what kind of animal are you?
I've never seen anything
like you on land,
SEA OR ZOO."

"Hi, I am Haley-Ann and
I come from Planet Pong,
I've come to visit
Earth,
to find the friend for
whom I long."

Haley-Ann thought Humphrey
looked **stranger** than her,
What with his long neck,
two humps and all covered in fur.

Suddenly Haley-Ann backfired and
Humphrey started to run!

"STOP!"
shouted Haley-Ann,
"I can't help doing
what I've done!"

He hid behind a cactus shaking,
nervous and all hot.
"What was that noise?
I thought that I'd been **shot!**"

Haley-Ann replied,
"Sorry I scared you and
made you jump,
Sometimes when I'm excited,
I do a little trump!"

He emerged
from behind the cactus saying,
"OK, I understand!
I know it was an accident and
not something you had planned."

Both smiled and played for
hours
while on the warm sand dune.
Then night-time fell and
Haley-Ann dreamt under the
stars and moon.

Humphrey became Haley-Ann's
one true
and very special mate.

The only problem was when Haley-Ann's
backside decided to deflate!

This is how
an alien had a camel for her best friend,

They'd have more adventures,

but for now it's the **end**!